# THE DAY THE SCHEDULE BROKE

Sandra (not Sandy, Sands or Sando) pushed a stack of papers aside, then cursed as it overbalanced and slipped off her wonky desk in a cascading flurry of individual sheets across the floor.

She leaned across to her left and looked around her desk at the once organised, colour coded, sticky noted, highlighted and marked-up schedule pages currently strewn haphazardly across the tiny area of worn grey carpet not currently stacked with racks of boxes of props and equipment.

It was the kind of filing crisis that would take twice as long to reorder as it would to reprint. And version control be damned, very tempting to simply sweep it into a corner under the racking and leave it to gather dust like the crushed and torn boxes stored within them.

Her tiny basement office, dimly lit by one small street-level window (and a bare flickering light globe) was literally a storage cupboard before she moved in.

Technically, it still was a storage cupboard, though she wasn't entirely sure whether she was leftover junk in storage or not.

Her pay still landed neatly and on time in her bank account, suggesting not mothballed, but the room's damp, musty smell of forgotten dreams and hopes contended she was in storage.

Or perhaps some kind of black hole event horizon she couldn't escape was a better description.

Frozen in time and place.

She pushed her chair back, and in doing so, knocked the desk off its chock of exactly two and a half pads of sticky notes.

And set in motion a Rube Goldberg style chain reaction of levers and ratchets and spinning wheels and falling things that resulted in a box of light reflectors resettling at precisely the right angle to cast the mess on the floor and dust motes floating in the air in a magical golden glow.

Something clockwork, somewhere in the storage rack started ticking rapidly for a moment, before slowing down, getting slower and slower and finally stopped leaving the room still and silent.

# THE DAY THE SCHEDULE BROKE

A SHORT STORY

ALEXANDRIA BLAELOCK

BlueMere Books
MELBOURNE, AUSTRALIA

For permission requests, please contact
enquiries@bluemerebooks.com.

Ordering Information:
Discounts are available on quantity purchases. For details, contact orders@bluemerebooks.com.

The Say the Schedule Brole/Alexandria Blaelock
paperback ISBN: 978-1-925749-45-8
digital ISBN: 978-1-925749-46-5

Book Layout © BookDesignTemplates.com

Worse, in some undefinable way than it had been before.

Like her time had run out.

Sandra sighed.

Some days started bad and just got worse.

She started quietly muttering swear words, cursing the day she'd agreed to take up the Project Scheduler contract with Gorgon Studios.

No, not just that.

Maybe as far back as her first job with Con.

Con by name, con by nature.

Was that far enough back? Or should it be the first day she met him?

A chance encounter leading to her first project role, the start of a successful project career, and finally here, now in this pathetic excuse for an office, full of broken-down rubbish, working with a bunch of morons.

Surely that was enough now.

Surely it was time to move on to some other job where she had a habitable place to work and was treated with a little respect.

Was it not?

She made a grab for her bag and jacket hanging on the old fashioned hat stand (also broken), but they were caught up in the hooks, and the whole thing fell towards her making her jump and dance to avoid losing an eye and tearing an arm off her jacket in the process.

Forgetting its old-fashioned wooden solidity, she kicked the prostrate rack, hurting herself and probably scoring a massive bruise across her shin too.

Another string of curse words - just as well she had an "office" to herself and didn't have to contribute to anyone else's swear jar.

She picked her handbag out of the wreckage and left the cupboard, slamming the door behind her.

As she walked away, down the dim corridor, she heard something(s) crashing as it fell from the racks.

She paused for a moment, debating whether to go back and see what, then squared her shoulders, and kept walking, with no intention of returning.

No matter how curious she was about whether the door would actually open, or whether some brooding and unhappy presence had barricaded itself in.

Or her out.

Or whether she'd shot through the event horizon and out the other side into a universe very like the one she'd left only different in some way that wasn't readily apparent but would come to a horrifying conclusion over the next few weeks.

Honestly, the sooner she got back into less creative projects, the better. Something a little less creative and a little more stable and predictable.

Like construction.

But on her way off the lot, a sharp pain in her stomach reminded her she hadn't eaten in hours.

She stood still for a moment, one hand on her stomach trying to decide whether she could make it to the bus stop before passing out from hunger.

The lovely Art Deco café building on the main entrance to the back lot operated as an actual cafe, as well as a set, so she figured she might as well stop in on her way out and get herself one last discounted lunch.

To go.

But by the time she collected her chicken noodle soup and toasted ham and cheese sandwich, she knew she couldn't wait any longer, and found herself a sunbeam on the portico of a nearby building (currently dressed as a post office) to eat her sandwich.

She leaned back on a white painted pillar, stretched out her red denim jean clad legs, and tugged her white fitted button-down shirt down to a more comfortable fitting.

She couldn't remember which project was filming right now - something involving a pretty blonde boy and some kind of mixed martial arts fighting, currently rehearsing in and around a "bank" on the other side of the street.

Or maybe it was a shop.

They were still dressing the exterior, so it was hard to tell.

The men weren't fighting particularly fiercely, but the random sounds of grunting and limbs connecting was irritating and disturbing her attempt at calming herself sufficiently not to tear the head off the next person who spoke to her.

She pulled her phone and earbuds from their respective pockets in her handbag and plugged herself into something a little more calming and soothing.

Well, given it was a Stravinsky ballet, more like something loud and clashing, cleansing and cathartic.

It certainly added an unexpectedly dramatic dimension to the fight scene unfolding in front of her.

Though of course, it was carefully choreographed, which was why they were rehearsing.

And they were rehearsing for a movie, so what she was watching would come out something similar on the other side anyway.

But probably with a soundtrack leaning more towards the heavy metal end of the musical spectrum.

And when you thought about it, movies took a collection of singularly ordinary moments, shone a bit of gold light on them and undercut them with a bit of dramatic music and made them seem more exceptional than they really were.

Larger than life.

About six times larger on the smallest of theatre screens actually.

As many as thirty times on the larger.

Sandra closed her eyes, took a deep breath and held it for ten seconds before letting it out again.

She loosened the lid on her soup to let the steam out and give it some time to cool while she started eating her sandwich.

From her vantage point, Pretty Boy's fluid fighting style included the odd stylish gesture; he seemed sweet and wholesome, and she guessed he was playing the hero.

His dark-haired opponent's style was sparer and more calculated, suggesting a lethal efficiency, and she guessed he was the villain.

Despite herself, she was intrigued, and wondered why it was that she preferred the villain. Was it a kindred recognition of a different kind of precision to her own?

Or was it the sense that heroes live in a slightly parallel universe of sunshine and unceasing positivity, while villains see the universe for the miserable, dark place it is.

Was it possible the villain and hero were different sides of the same coin - light and dark, locked forever in mortal combat that neither of them would ever win?

The same guy spinning endlessly in battle with his own shadow.

Or more likely, it was time to give Stravinsky a break and listen to something more cheerful.

She shook her head to dispel her thoughts, and as she did, a drop of fat from her sandwich escaped the paper it was wrapped in and dripped onto her shirt.

She held her arms out to the side as she looked down on her chest.

Just bloody perfect.

Not only would everyone be staring at her breasts for the rest of the day, but she'd be tormented by the smell of toasted cheese.

And of course, she'd ruined her jacket so unless she went back to her office, tore the other arm off it, and wore it backwards, she was stuck like this.

And just when she thought her day couldn't get any worse, the fighting crossed the street, and Pretty Boy tripped over her outstretched legs and somehow kicked her soup all over her shirt too.

Unbelievable day.

"What the hell do you think you are doing?" he demanded. "Can't you see we're rehearsing here?"

After a moment of incredulity, Sandra struggled to her feet, flicking hot soup from her hands, before scraping it off her top, and accidentally on purpose flicking it in his direction.

"Actually," she said, crossing her arms over her nearly transparent shirt, "if you were rehearsing according to the approved protocols, you would have cleared the area, installed warning placards and the authorised safety barriers to prevent incidents like this.

"Clearly you're not rehearsing, you've just crossed the street to assault me."

Pretty Boy performed an unnecessarily flamboyant backflip back to his feet while Sandra took a step closer to the edge of the portico, to prevent him from stepping up to her level and towering over her.

He was tall enough as he was thank you very much.

She wondered if she remembered enough Taekwondo to get herself out of trouble, and as she thought about it, relaxed into position ready to strike.

As if in recognition, a hand fell on her shoulder at the same moment as a male voice from behind her said, "Oh my god, I'm so sorry about Jason, are you okay?"

She twisted out from under the hand and found herself face to chest with the villain, who was looking down into her face.

On the bright side, the cheese stain was indistinguishable from the soup stains, and he was looking at her face, not her chest.

She took a step back along the edge of the step, trying to maintain a safe distance from both of them, but the villain took a step closer to bridge the gap.

On the bright side, he was between her and Pretty Boy, or Jason, or whatever the hell his name was, and on the less bright side, he was still looking at her.

Sandra brought her feet together and stood as tall as she could without standing on her toes, "I'm fine, though it seems I am destined to be hungry today."

It seemed she might also be destined to never regain her composure.

"I don't know what you're apologising for Dan," Pretty Boy said, "placard schmacard, we have every right to be here."

Without breaking eye contact with her, Dan held up the palm of his hand back in Jason's direction.

"No, she's right. You could've been injured, and that could have delayed the shoot. Next time we'll do it properly."

She had the curious feeling Dan was trying to protect Pretty Boy from her.

While the thought she might capable of damaging him was amusing, it was just another reminder of how much working at Gorgon Studios sucked.

The only reason movie stars thought the world revolved around them was that for three months of filming it actually did.

They had to be kept happy so they didn't interrupt the schedule, that time and cost could be controlled, and hopefully, The Project brought in on time and on budget.

She sighed.

That was what she managed the schedules for after all.

That was why they all took care of the stars because with their faces plastered all over the screens, they were more or less irreplaceable for the duration whereas every other one of them was expendable.

She turned her back on Dan and picked up her bag and collected the remains of her lunch, "you take care of The Star, I'll get someone to clean up."

Back straight, head high, she walked away from the jerks.

Stopping to throw the remains of her lunch in a bin, and at the gatehouse to ask Sol to call for a cleaner, and then at the bus stop until a bus arrived.

Exit stage right.

《《 • 》》

Dan watched the girl go.

She was magnificent.

He'd been worried for a moment when Jason opened his stupid mouth, and he recognised her Taekwondo relax.

Though if he had to lay a bet on the outcome, her lightness and speed would've seen Jason rolling on the ground with a broken nose.

And the last thing they needed was a hero with a broken nose. Heroes were supposed to be pretty and virtuous, not scarred for life.

If they were being honest, Jason wasn't smart enough to play a villain, and he wasn't nice enough for anyone to take a chance on him - when he lost his looks, he'd lose his career as well.

Assuming the drugs didn't kill it first.

But that was Jason's problem, not his.

Though the idea of that girl, whoever she was, ending his career was delicious.

With a few weeks of filming left, there was enough time to come up with an idea of how he could make it happen.

He wouldn't be the only one happy to see Jason taken down a few pegs.

For the next few days, everywhere he went on the lot, he looked for her with no success.

He was reduced to asking questions, and after a while, he discovered Sandra Lockwood was one of the Studio schedulers.

And seemingly a very good one.

People who worked with her praised her efficiency and can-do attitude. People who didn't talked about how polite she was and how pleasant to be around.

So far as Dan could tell, the only person who had anything bad to say about her was Jason, which was as good a recommendation as any.

But apparently, she'd been ill, and no one had seen her for a while.

Once he knew who she was, it was easy to find her office. And once he'd seen her office, it was easy to see why she was ill.

Though Dan suspected there was more to it than just that.

What few knew, was that with 52% ownership, Dan was Gorgon Studios' senior partner.

He'd set up the studios with some help from his friends, primarily as a way to ensure he had work. And when he didn't, he at least had some money coming in.

They'd started out small, bought some derelict factories, hired some incredibly gifted people, and grown into a sought-after provider of backlot, sound stages, props and production services.

And given most people are nervous around bosses, especially more senior ones, Dan preferred to keep his ownership a secret because he got better results that way.

The question became, how did he get Sandra back to work where he could spend time with her without her knowing he was technically her boss.

And one of the stars of the movie, which might be even worse.

It seemed the best way was to check on her using the Jason incident as an excuse.

Which was how he came to be knocking on her apartment door with a bunch of flowers.

And when she opened the door, she really did look ill.

Pale face, limp hair, dark panda eyes.

Dan wasn't sure whether to hold his arms out to catch her or call an ambulance.

He held out the flowers instead.

She looked at them, she looked at him, and then shrugged and took them out of his hands and walked back inside.

But she didn't shut the door in his face, so he closed the door behind him.

The warm clove-scented room he followed her into was small, neat and clean. Plain white shelves disappeared into the white walls so that the few books and brightly coloured ornaments on display appeared to float in the air.

It was stark, but it was also strangely relaxing.

No extraneous clutter, nothing to suggest any other occupants.

Even the bright orange blanket she'd probably climbed out from underneath looked like art thrown back against the square deep blue couch it rested on.

Not to mention the low black lacquerware table.

Her dark, disorganised office must be a daily torture compared to this open and organised space.

"I heard you were ill," he said, "and I was worried Jason had hurt you."

He thought he heard her snort, but her head was in a cupboard so he couldn't say for sure.

She came out with a large vase and some scissors and started trimming the flowers to fit the vase.

"Not physically," she replied, "it was just one of those days."

"Why, what happened?"

She smiled slightly, "too stupid to go into."

Her eyes met his for a moment before bouncing away.

"Are you okay, you seem..." he waved his arms his vaguely, not wanting to say the words out loud.

She bent her face towards the flowers and sniffed them, the reds and yellows reflecting a healthy glow onto her face.

"I'm just tired."

"I called by your office, so I'm not surprised you're tired."

She frowned.

"Well, you live here, and the place you work couldn't be more different than this."

She looked around her as if she'd only just made the connection.

"I suppose that's true."

"When I get back to the lot, I'll tell them to clear the space up."

"Don't bother, I'm not planning to go back."

"You're not going to quit over Jason are you?"

"What? No, not him. He's just the last straw."

"Then what?"

"It's just time to move on."

"Surely there's more to it than that?"

"Yes. No. Oh, I don't know. The idea of returning just fills me with despair."

"Despair? That seems like a fairly strong reaction."

"You said you saw my office, right?"

He took a step towards her, "give me a chance to set this right."

"Give you a chance? I think you might be giving yourself a little too much credit, don't you?"

"I'm sorry, I feel like this is all my fault for letting Jason get out of control—"

She folded her arms across her chest, "I told you this isn't about Jason."

He risked another step forward, "then what?"

She looked at him for a long moment, and he thought she was going to throw him out with some choice words.

She sighed and sort of collapsed in on herself, "it just feels like this is one of those points where life could go either way. That the rest of my life depends on this decision."

Despite himself, he was intrigued. "this would be something related to your Taekwondo training?"

She laughed, "ah, you saw that did you?"

"I did. I would've put money on you to win - that's why I had to intervene."

"That's flattering, I guess.

"And yes, my mind is not at peace."

"Would you like to tell me about it? I can't promise wise counsel, but it might help you clarify your thoughts."

She did her Taekwondo relax for a moment as she stared at him for an eternity, before asking, "would you like some tea?"

Of course he nodded.

She didn't say anything as she boiled the kettle and prepared the tea things. She put them on a tray, and carried it over to the table, gesturing for him to sit as she knelt before the table and poured the tea.

She waited for him to take his first sip, and then she started talking.

He watched her face move as she spoke and admired the sparkle in her dark eyes.

A lock of her fringe fell forward and caught in her eyebrow, and he admired its tenacity.

He noticed her square, even teeth, and her thin pale lips.

And the less he listened to her words, and the more he admired her look, the more he understood that she was bored at work, and felt under-appreciated.

That she felt some guy had used their friendship, and ultimately her to achieve his own goals.

That she was better than this, and deserved more, but didn't quite know what she needed to do to get there.

Now and again, he poured her more tea and admired the economy of her movements as she drank it.

And couldn't help wondering how that would translate to her bedroom before forcing himself back to the matter at hand.

Eventually, she ran out of words.

He said nothing.

She reached into the sleeve of her shirt, pulled out a scrunched-up tissue and blew her nose.

"How do you feel?" he asked.

She smiled, "better."

"Want some advice?"

"No. But I'll give you a second chance."

"Me?"

"I know who you are Daniel Carruthers, movie star and Gorgon Studios CEO."

"Ah," he laughed a little nervously.

"I'll be back at work next week. Show me what you've got."

《《 • 》》

Sandra stood across the road, looking at the studio's main entrance.

There was nothing obviously different, but there was some kind of subtle change in the air.

A kind of lightness.

Not cheerfulness exactly, but a kind of airiness.

Like after a thunderstorm when the first few sunbeams shine through the departing clouds.

Clean and bright.

Or maybe it was just her.

The café seemed livelier, and her takeout latte was delivered in her reusable cup with a smiley face drawn on the lid.

As she made her way across the lot, she was surprised and touched by the number of people who stopped to greet her, to tell her they'd missed seeing her about the place and were glad she was back.

She'd never felt like a part of the placed before.

No sign of Dan though.

Not sure whether she was glad about that or not.

Not that she was looking, she told herself.

Her corridor looked the same, her office door looked the same.

Maybe a little cleaner.

She put her hand on the knob and paused before turning it, but she had no sense of an unhappy brooding presence.

She flung the door open and was confronted by clean white walls.

The window had been replaced, and the new one was not only clean but open a crack to let fresh air in and the hint of fresh paint out.

Under the window, an orange couch snuggled with a blue rug under a silver-coloured lamp stand topped with a white shade.

And behind the couch, a large, framed, orange-tinted movie poster for *The Day the Schedule Broke,* starring Sandra Lockwood and Dan Carruthers. It showed Dan crouching before a taller, somewhat menacing version of her, arms spread wide in defence of a cowering Jason.

It reminded her a little of the original *Attack of the 50 ft Woman* poster.

To her left, the racking remained, though painted white, and aside from some files and empty space, it contained several bright green plants in white pots.

On her right, diagonally opposite the door, a long, pale wood table took up almost the entire wall. One end was topped with neat stacks of colour coded, sticky noted, highlighted and marked-up schedule pages, the other held a new black computer and printer.

And in the middle, a wide-open space for laying out the plans. Under the desk, under the stacks of paper, was a low lateral filing cabinet.

A wheeled office chair, matching the orange couch sat between the table and the wall, giving her easy access to the long whiteboard hung on the wall, currently showing a Gantt chart of the main studio schedule.

She took a step into the room and shut the door.

Behind the door, a coat rack was screwed to the wall. And on the rack, in a plastic dry-cleaning shroud, hung a jacket. It looked a lot like her old jacket, with the sleeve sewn back on.

She smiled.

The room was perfect.

And she wondered if all that space had been there all along, or if Dan'd moved the walls.

She hung her bag and the jacket she was wearing on the rack, turned her computer on, and sat swinging from side to side on the new chair, sipping her coffee, while she waited for a gazillion new emails to download.

But she found herself distracted by the movie poster, and took her coffee to stand in front of it, examining it closely.

Jason's screwed up terrified face, Dan's dropped jaw and wide, staring eyes, her own scowling face as she waved a sandwich menacingly at the puny creatures cowering before her. A tiny overturned bowl of soup on the steps.

It was ingenious, and to be honest, a bit flattering too.

"So how did I do?" he asked from behind her.

"I love it," she said, turning around, arm brushing across his chest as she found him closer than expected.

And dressed better, in a dark suit, shirt and tie.

"Wrapping up filming?"

"Nah, board meeting."

She snorted, "you look nice."

"Nice enough to take you out for a drink?"

"I just got here! And it's not even lunchtime yet."

"You're late. And it's nearly lunchtime. Though I should get back to the meeting."

He held a hand out to her, "meet later?"

Surprising herself as well as him, she took his hand, "okay."

He held her gaze for a moment before kissing the back of her hand, "I'll look forward to it."

She blushed like a schoolgirl as she watched him leave, his aftershave lingering behind him.

Didn't seem like she'd broken his schedule, though hers might never recover.

She bounced on the balls of her feet a few times, before jumping and spinning, and lashing out into the empty space with a head-height kick.

It seemed things were taking a turn for the better.

She couldn't wait to see him again.

## THE END

Alexandria Blaelock writes stories, some of them for *Ellery Queen's Mystery Magazine* and *Pulphouse Fiction Magazine*. She's also written four self-help books applying business techniques to personal matters like getting dressed, cleaning house, and feeding your friends.

As a recovering Project Manager, she's probably too fond of sticking to plan. She lives in a forest because she enjoys birdsong, the scent of gum leaves and the sun on her face. When not telecommuting to parallel universes from her Melbourne based imagination, she watches K-dramas, talks to animals, and drinks Campari. At the same time.

Discover more at www.alexandriablaelock.com.

# OTHER SHORT STORIES BY ALEXANDRIA BLAELOCK

Alma's Grace
Balancing the Book
Bygone Boyfriend
Carmelita Basingstoke
Fate in Your Hands
Kiss of Death
Lady of the Looking Glass
Life in the Security Directorate
Long Weekend in the Snow
Love in the Security Directorate
Morning Star, Evening Star, Superstar
Needy Bitch
Payton's Run
Phoenix Child
Secret Singer
Shining Star
Ship in a Bottle
Simone Says Hands in the Air
The Day the Schedule Broke
The Guardian's Vigil
Toy Soldiers

# BOOKS BY ALEXANDRIA BLAELOCK

## FICTION

That Love Nonsense

## MS BLAELOCK'S BOOKS

Stress Free Dinner Parties
Signature Wardrobe Planning
Holistic Personal Finance
Minimally Viable Housekeeping